Pirate Pete's
Talk Like a Pirate

Pirate Pete's Talk Like a Pirate

by Kim Kennedy *illustrated by* Doug Kennedy

SCHOLASTIC INC.
New York Toronto London Auckland Sydney
Mexico City New Delhi Hong Kong Buenos Aires

Pirate Pete had the most amazing ship ever to sail the high seas, but he needed a crew. Not any old crew would do, however.

"I needs me a pirate crew," Pete told his parrot. "And I know just where to find one: Rascal Island!"

"To Rascal Island we go!" cried the bird.

Pete spun the wheel toward the Sea of Mischief,
and soon his speedy ship had reached Rascal Island.

Pete dropped anchor in the bay, and then he hung a sign across the ship's bow: BUCCANEERS WANTED.

Before long, a boat filled with rascals rowed up to the ship. Pete rubbed his hands in glee! They were the dirtiest, most mischievous, and sneakiest-looking scallywags and scurvy dogs he'd ever laid his eye on.

One by one, the rascals climbed aboard the ship.

"Listen up, mateys!" announced the parrot. "If ye wants to sail with Pete, then ye've gots to prove ye gots what it takes!"

Pete nodded and declared,
"Ye needs a peg leg and an ol' eye patch,
A fierce-lookin' hook and a beard ye can scratch!
Ye gots to load a cannon and know how to fire it,
But most of all, ye gots to talk like a pirate!"

A rascal stepped forward, loaded the cannon, and fired it.
"Nice firin'!" said Pete. "And I sees ye gots a peg leg, hook, and eye patch. And that beard of yours . . . does it hanker for a scratch?"
"It *is* quite itchy," answered the man. "Especially during the summer, when the weather tends to be sultry."

"Blow me down!" bellowed Pete. "Ye don't talk like a pirate! Walk the plank!"

As the man splashed overboard, Pete hollered,
"Ye should've said,
'When the sun's a-blazin',
Me beard gets the itches,
Worse than a bucket of sand down me britches!'"

"Next!" ordered the parrot.

Pete squinted at the rest of the rascals and said,
"Ye gots to be stubborn and mighty cranky,
Ye gots to be dirty and awfully stanky!
Ye gots to load a cannon and know how to fire it,
But most of all, ye gots to talk like a pirate!"

A rascal stepped forward, loaded the cannon, and fired it.
"Nice firin'!" said Pete. "And I see that yer plenty dirty and stanky. But is ye stubborn and cranky?"

"Oh, indeed!" replied the rascal. "Sometimes I'm very irritable, especially when I don't eat my breakfast."

"Shiver me timbers!" shouted Pete. "Ye don't talk like a pirate! Walk the plank!"

As the rascal went overboard, Pete cried,
"Ye should've said,
'I's as mean as a shark
That's stuck in a tub,
When I've not scarfed me mornin' grub!'"

"Next!" squawked the bird.

Pete glared at the rascals and said,
"Ye gots to love treasure! Why, it's your duty
To plunder ship and shore for gleamin' booty!
Ye gots to load a cannon and know how to fire it,
But most of all, ye gots to talk like a pirate!"

A rascal stepped forward, loaded the cannon, and fired it.
"Nice firin'!" said Pete. "And judgin' by the gold and rubies yer flauntin', I reckon ye've done some plunderin' in yer day."
"That is correct," said the rascal. "I've misappropriated a number of fine jewels without permission."
"Blimey!" cried Pete. "Ye don't talk like a pirate! Walk the plank!"

As the rascal leaped overboard, Pete shouted,
"Ye should've said,
'I've pilfered loot on land and at sea,
And no man's say-so has ever stopped me!'"

"Next!" blared the parrot.

Pete shook his head. He had finally lost his patience. He curled up his lip at the last rascal and declared,

"Ye gots to trim the sails and mind the deck,
Ye gots to be brave in case of shipwreck,
Ye gots to load a cannon and know how to fire it,
But most of all, ye gots to talk like a pirate!"

The rascal walked forward, loaded the cannon, and fired it.

"Nice firin'!" said Pete. "But is ye brave? 'Cause no lily-livered seafarer is gonna sail with me!"

"I can *assure* you that I am extremely courageous," said the rascal. "I will conduct myself with valor at all times."

"Confound it!" shouted Pete, stomping his foot. "Ye don't talk like a pirate! Walk the plank!"

As the rascal dropped overboard, Pete yelled,
"Ye should've said,
'I've not a yellow-bellied bone
From me head to me toes.
I'll stand brave upon this ship wherever she goes!'"

"Can ye believe it?" Pete moaned to his parrot. "Out of all them rascals, not a one was fit for me crew."

"'Tis true!" squawked the bird. "By the powers! They's no more than a bunch o' squiffies and sprogs! None of 'em fit to go a-swashbucklin' and plunderin' for pieces of eight upon the briney blue on this here vessel!"

Pete blinked.

"Why, ye talk just like a pirate!" he cheered to the bird. "Yer all the crew I needs. Weigh anchor!"

"Aye, aye," said the parrot, and off they sailed.

Back to the high seas went Pete and his bird.
A pirate always gets the last word!
They looked for a crew so they could hire it,
But blimey, none could talk like a pirate!

For Jackson
—Doug

For Dan
—Kim

ISBN-13: 978-0-545-06951-9
ISBN-10: 0-545-06951-3

Published by Scholastic Inc., 557 Broadway, New York, NY 10012,
by arrangement with Abrams Books for Young Readers,
an imprint of Harry N. Abrams, Inc.

12 11 10 9 8 7 6 5 4 3 2 1 8 9 10 11 12 13/0

Printed in the U.S.A. 08

First Scholastic printing, February 2008

Book design by Vivian Cheng